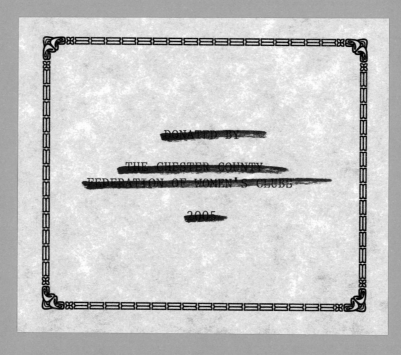

Babu's Song

by **Stephanie Stuve-Bodeen**

illustrated by **Aaron Boyd**

Lee & Low Books Inc.
New York

Lee & Low Books Inc., 95 Madison Avenue, New York, NY 10016
leeandlow.com

Manufactured in China by South China Printing Co.

Book Design by Tania Garcia
Book Production by The Kids at Our House

The text is set in New Baskerville
The illustrations are rendered in watercolor

10 9 8 7 6 5 4 3 2 1
First Edition

Library of Congress Cataloging-in-Publication Data
Stuve-Bodeen, Stephanie.
    Babu's song / by Stephanie Stuve-Bodeen ; illustrated by Aaron Boyd.—
1st ed.
        p. cm.
    Summary: In Tanzania, Bernardi's mute grandfather makes him a wonderful
music box and then helps him realize his dream of owning a soccer ball and
going to school.
    ISBN 1-58430-058-2
    [1. Grandfathers—Fiction. 2. Schools—Fiction. 3. Soccer—Fiction. 4. Music
box—Fiction. 5. Mute persons—Fiction. 6. People with disabilities—Fiction.
7. Blacks—Tanzania—Fiction. 8. Tanzania—Fiction] I. Boyd, Aaron, ill. II. Title.
PZ7.S9418 Bab 2003
[E]—dc21   2002067130

Bernardi ran hard, kicking the ball toward the goal. His arms pumping and his heart racing, he didn't care that he was the only boy on the field not wearing a school uniform. He loved soccer and his one concern was making a goal. With a final kick so powerful that it knocked him on his back, Bernardi sent the ball flying past the goalie and into the net.

Bernardi lay on the grassy field, catching his breath.
A boy helped him up, then ran after the others going
into the school. Bernardi wished he could go to school
like the other children. He liked to learn, and thought
he could be a good student. Besides, then he could play
soccer every day, not just when the schoolboys needed
an extra player. Bernardi lived with his grandfather,
Babu, and they did not have enough money for school.
    Slowly Bernardi walked home.

When Bernardi walked in, Babu gave him a hug. This was how he said hello, because an illness had taken his voice a long time ago.

"Hello, Babu," Bernardi said. "I made a goal today." Bernardi loved telling Babu his soccer stories.

Babu held up a figure made of wood. He pulled a string, and the figure's jointed arms and legs popped up and down, making Bernardi laugh. Babu was a toy maker. He had only to look at an object and he knew what toy it would become, such as an airplane from a tin can or a whistle from a scrap of wood.

After Babu made his toys Bernardi would sell them. Together they made enough money to live on.

Babu made tea for Bernardi and himself. After they finished Bernardi took an old bag from beside the door, waved good-bye to Babu, and set off for the market. As he walked, Bernardi hummed a tune. It was a song that Babu had sung when he had his voice. Humming it made Bernardi wish Babu could still speak.

"Anything for Babu?" Bernardi asked the vendors when he reached the market.

The vendors gave Bernardi bits of string or paper, anything that Babu might be able to use to make his toys. Mama Valentina, who sold salt, called to Bernardi. She handed him a plastic gunnysack. Bernardi thanked her as he stuffed it into his bag, even though he didn't think Babu could use it.

As Bernardi walked home, he passed a shop downtown and stopped to look in the window. There among the bright bolts of cloth and shiny pots was a new soccer ball. It was just what he had always wanted. Bernardi pressed his face against the window and looked at the price. It was more than it cost to go to school!

Slowly Bernardi backed away from the window. He did not hum as he walked home.

That evening Babu and Bernardi ate beans and rice by the light of the kerosene lamp. Babu put something by Bernardi's plate. Bernardi picked it up and held it closer to the light. It looked like a tin of lard. He opened the lid and heard a small tinkling.

"A music box!" Bernardi exclaimed, and listened again. It was rough and tinny, but he recognized the tune. It was Babu's song.

Bernardi hugged Babu, and together they listened to the music. That night, for the first time in many nights, Bernardi fell asleep listening to Babu's song.

The next Saturday was a busy one for
Bernardi, as it was the day he sold toys to
tourists. He set up shop on his favorite
corner downtown, arranging the toys on
the curb.

Bernardi cranked the music box and
listened to Babu's song tinkle out. He had
sold a few things when a woman picked
up the music box. She asked how much it
was, but Bernardi said it wasn't for sale.

The woman did not give up. She told Bernardi that she wanted the music box for her collection, but still Bernardi shook his head. The woman held out a handful of money. Bernardi's eyes widened. It would be more than enough to buy the ball in the store window!

Bernardi picked up the music box. He thought about the brand-new ball and how it would feel when he kicked it. Surely Babu could make another music box.

Bernardi swallowed hard and took the money.

After Bernardi sold all the toys he did not go home. He took the money and headed for the shops down the street.

When Bernardi got home, Babu was cleaning. He looked up at Bernardi holding the empty bag. "I sold everything, Babu!" Bernardi said, trying to sound cheerful, but then a tear rolled down his face. Babu went over to Bernardi. He wiped his grandson's face and waited. He knew Bernardi would tell him what was wrong.

Bernardi sniffled. He told Babu about the music box and the soccer ball. Then he handed the money to Babu. "I couldn't buy the ball, Babu. It's your money."

Babu patted Bernardi's head. Then he placed the money in Bernardi's hand and held it, to show him that the money belonged to both of them.

Bernardi hung his head. "I don't want the ball anymore." He held out the money. "Take it, Babu. You decide what to do with the money."

Babu took the money and looked thoughtfully at Bernardi for a long time. Then he broke into a smile, signaled to Bernardi to wait, and walked out the door.

Bernardi sat quietly in the room as he waited for Babu. He wished he still had the music box. How could he have sold it?

Bernardi was sitting in the lamplight when Babu returned holding a paper bag. Babu pulled out a package and handed it to Bernardi.

Bernardi choked back a sob. He untied the string and pulled back the brown paper. His eyes opened wide when he saw what was inside. It was a school uniform!

Bernardi looked at Babu. "You paid for me to go to school?"

Babu nodded. Bernardi jumped up and hugged his grandfather.

While Bernardi held the new uniform to his chest, Babu went back outside. He returned holding something behind his back. With a flourish Babu held out a soccer ball made from string and Mama Valentina's gunnysack.

Bernardi put down his uniform and held the ball. He bounced it on one knee and it felt like the real thing.

"Thank you, Babu. It's wonderful!" Bernardi said to his grandfather and gave him a hug. Babu beamed. Bernardi decided that the ball was even better than the real thing.

Babu pulled one more surprise from the paper bag.
It was an empty lard tin. As Babu began to make another
music box, Bernardi put the water on the stove to boil.
Then Bernardi hummed Babu's song as they sat in the
lamplight and waited for their tea.